Clap Your Hands

Lorinda Bryan Cauley

HARCOURT BRACE & COMPANY
Orlando   Atlanta   Austin   Boston   San Francisco   Chicago   Dallas   New York
Toronto   London

This edition is published by special arrangement with G. P. Putnam's Sons,
a division of The Putnam & Grosset Group.

Grateful acknowledgment is made to G. P. Putnam's Sons, a division of
The Putnam & Grosset Group for permission to reprint *Clap Your Hands*
by Lorinda Bryan Cauley. Copyright © 1992 by Lorinda Bryan Cauley.

Printed in the United States of America

ISBN 0-15-307391-8

1 2 3 4 5 6 7 8 9 10   026   99 98 97 96

To my little girls, Sean and Erin

Clap your hands,
stomp your feet.

Shake your arms,
then take a seat.

Rub your tummy,
pat your head.

Find something yellow,
find something red.

Reach for the sky,
wiggle your toes.

Stick out your tongue
and touch your nose.

Roar like a lion,
growl like a bear.

Give me a kiss . . .
Do you dare?

Wiggle your fingers,
slap your knee.

I'll tickle you
if you tickle me!

Find something big,
find something small.

Spin in a circle . . .
but try not to fall!

Close your eyes
and count to four.

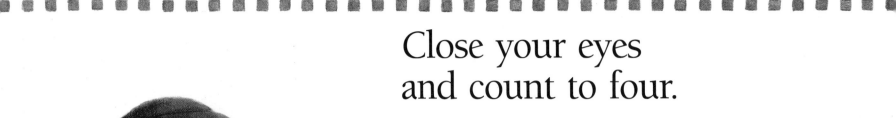

Now do a somersault
across the floor.

Spread your feet,
look upside down.

Make a silly face
and act like
a clown.

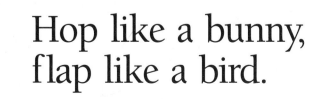

Hop like a bunny,
flap like a bird.

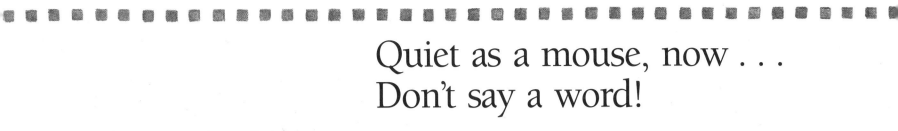

Quiet as a mouse, now . . .
Don't say a word!

Tell me your name.
How old are you?

Tell me a secret,
and I'll tell you one, too!

Purr like a kitten,
bark like a dog.

Crawl like a baby,
jump like a frog.

25

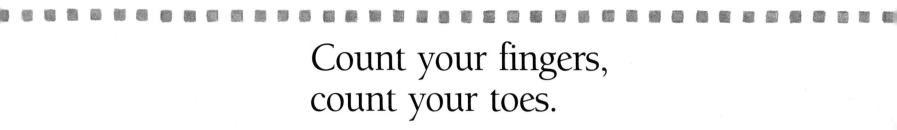

Count your fingers,
count your toes.

Wiggle your eyebrows,
wiggle your nose.

Show me a smile,
show me a frown.

Stand on one foot
and jump up
and down.

Fly like an airplane
high in the sky.

It's time to go now,
so wave bye-bye . . .

Bye-bye!